The Earliest Patriots

The Earliest Patriots
Being the true Adventures of certain survivors of 'Bussa's Rebellion' (1816), in the island of Barbados and Abroad

by Evelyn O'Callaghan
Introduction by Hilary Beckles

Karia Press

The Earliest Patriots:
Being the true adventures of certain
survivors of 'Bussa's Rebellion' (1816),
in the island of Barbados and Abroad

First published by **Karia Press** in 1986.
Copyright © Evelyn O'Callaghan
Copyright © Introduction Hilary Beckles

Cover design by Buzz Johnson.

ISBN 0 946918 53 8 Pb

Karia Press,
BCM Karia,
London, WC1N 3XX.

Made and printed in Great Britain by the
Guernsey Press Co. Ltd., Guernsey, Channel Islands.

Contents

Introduction by Hilary Beckles 9

The Earliest Patriots:
Being the true adventures of certain
survivors of 'Bussa's Rebellion' (1816),
in the island of Barbados and Abroad 13

Appendix 1.

From report of Select Committee of the House of Assembly
appointed to inquire into the Origin, Cases and Progress
of the late Insurrection, Barbados 1816 50

Appendix 2.

Report of the Commissioners of Inquiry into the state
of Sierra leone 7 May, 1927,
House of Commons, London. 53

Appendix 3

Statement of Samuel Lane — 6 March, 1926 55

Appendix 4.

Original letter from Exiled Barbadians to the
Queen Victoria (transcribed on P.39) 59

It broke out on two Plantations, belonging to the same Proprietor (a Mr. Scott); and it seems to have been for some time conceived that it was confined to them. To any one actually unacquainted with the Country, it must necessarily appear from the preceding extract, that these Estates of Mr. Scott were comprised within this narrow district, which is marked out as the area of the Insurrection. Now, how stands the fact itself? The Estates which belong to that Gentleman are situated in the Parish of St. Philip,—at its windward part, which is the most remote from the Parishes of Christ Church and St. George; so that the Slaves upon those and neighbouring Estates must have traversed (as they really did) the whole of that, the largest Parish in the Island, before they extended themselves into Christ Church and St. George.

It appears, by the accounts received from Barbadoes, that above twelve hundred Negroes have perished in the conflict, and more than forty estates have been totally (or the greatest part) destroyed by fire: the loss is computed at 250,000 sterling!

Introduction

In one of her most incisive critiques of recent Caribbean historical writing, the late Professor Elsa Goveia emphasised the need to recognise that 'the slave was, after all, and above all, a human being, and to obscure that fact is to obscure humanity itself.' The implication of this statement for scholars of history is far reaching. This is particularly so at present because there is a growing trend among historians to attempt the reconstruction of past realities by means of sophisticated statistical and mathematical models. Consequently, it has become necessary to ponder how this approach to historical writing obscures that invaluable humanity with which Goveia was principally concerned.

This work by Evelyn O'Callaghan is within the classical tradition where historical facts are blended with, or rooted within, fictional narratives aimed at the revelation of aspects of social experiences long buried beneath fragmented archival data. Its literary objective is to give life, character and identity to names which litter the crumbling pages of historical manuscripts. The persistent attractiveness of this method of historical writing, popularly known as 'faction', is that it combines close attention to fact with imaginative fiction, results from a rejection of the arid, technical writings which at present dominate historical science.

The narrative itself concerns an area of West Indian history which is of great philosophical significance—that of popular revolt against slavery. If it is true that a central characteristic of human history is the search for freedom from tyranny, then West Indian slaves with a tradition of revolt might have made their most notable contribution to a higher level of social civilization. By casting the narrative of slave life within the dynamics of rebellion, O'Callaghan shows the humanity of individuals that academic historians tend to obscure. It is a 'factional' account of the lives of some individuals who experienced the 1816 Barbados Slave Uprising. By basing the narrative upon documentary evidence, the author provides insights into the consciousness of slaves, an area which has remained blurred on account of historians' tendency to stay within the confines of literal data interpretation.

The origin of this work is located within years of editorial work which the author carried out on my manuscripts on Barbadian slave resistance. As such, she has more than a superficial familiarity with the raw data. Certain theoretical trends can be observed in the story—for example, an early pre-nationalist ideology can be identified among the slaves in spite of their masters' attempt to strip them of any sense of social, familial or geographical attachment. These slaves had loves, fears, values, life-objectives and, in spite of their enslavement, sought to develop these to their fullest. Their decision to revolt in April 1816, had much to do with the protection of these things. As such, this work, by revealing these aspects of human behaviour, is part of the overall critique of anti-humanist historiography outlined by Goveia. Indeed, it is within narratives like this that Black peoples' experiences as slaves in the New World are most sharply brought into focus.

Hilary Beckles
Department of History
University of the West Indies
Cave Hill Campus
Barbados

April, 1986

The Earliest Patriots
Being the true Adventures of certain survivors of 'Bussa's Rebellion' (1816), in the island of Barbados and Abroad

In late September of 1850, unseasonably heavy and protracted rains devasted the island of Barbados. The parish of St. Peter, and that of St. Philip, where I had resided for well nigh thirty-six years, were severely taxed by flooding. The young canes were drowned in a muddy-brown deluge, and everywhere there was a slope, violent streams churned seawards, bearing debris betokening the loss of livestock and property — a metal trunk, a bloated cow, sodden chickens. . . Everyday the rains fell, the situation worsened — it seemed the clements were truely at war with mankind! The scene that presented itself to me, from the refuge of my little cottage, which had fortunately escaped damage, was one of desolation. Not a soul was to be seen; all human life had disappeared off the face of the earth — an occurence which did not perturb me overly.

On the night of September twentieth, I sat alone and content in my sitting room, sipping a hot punch, and watching as the lightning flashes illuminated the sparsely furnished interior. Indeed, I chuckled to myself, I hardly require a fire with all the heavens provide! I confess the thunder unsettled me somewhat — it seemed as if there were devils abroad, cackling with joy at the cowardice of us paltry humans, shaking the very earth with their merriment!

Perhaps due to the inclemency of the weather, my thoughts turned, as they had not done for many months, to my home in Scotland. An old man, it is said, is wont to review his life and I suppose myself to be no exception, for now in my fifty-eighth year, I confess myself liable to such musings. 'Home' it could hardly be deemed *now,* I thought to myself, my contentment giving way to a familiar combination of bitterness and anger; for I had not returned to Scotland since I departed at twenty years of age, and 'home' it will never be. For I shall be buried here, in the grounds of the parish church (and not so long hence) — alone, unmourned, nay, as anonymous as I have sought to be these many years. I feel little affection for the place, I have no friends nor do I wish any. I have sufficient income from my practice, twice as much from the white patients as from the black; with the result that I live a comfortable though simple life, which is (I assure myself) admirably orderly, familiar and routine.

I take supper every few months with Mr. Gittens and his porcine wife, through habit rather than inclination, and for the rest of polite society, I leave them to their own devices. My medical colleagues are young dandies, scorning my old-fashioned theories; white creoles, most of them: a class, in my considered opinion, the most hypocritical, pompous and vulgar to be found in this corner of the world. I had enough to do with them in my early days in Barbados, and wish now for the minimum of social intercourse.

No, my dwelling here by the furthermost boundary of Refuge Plantation, far from the bustle of illustrious Barbadian society, is home enough for me; as long as I have solitude, rum and victuals enough, I am as well provided as any old man could wish.

It may have been the incessant rain which had called to mind my native land, for all my memories of that country are indeed grey and dour! The people of the region likewise appear — though mistily, now — as visions of grey and streaming faces, featureless beyond an impression of sourness, such as that engendered by the taste of a Jamaica lime. At the thought of Mister Gittens, at this juncture, I could not refrain from laughter, for *his* complexion, by contrast, was as florid as the infernal sun! The man was no favourite of mine, nor I his, yet we had served each other well enough.

I had been in his employ since I came to the island of Barbados in 1814, a stripling with no references from my previous employers in Jamaica. Indeed, I had arrived, as it were, 'under a cloud' — but Gittens asked no questions, and gave me the charge of his three hundred slaves at Refuge, and the care of his family, and, in time, those of neighbouring estates also requested my services. In this rural, isolated, yet well populated parish, few doctors chose to set up; thus I was able to supplement my income at Refuge with what I earned ministering to the slaves on certain other plantations. And indeed, I far preferred treating the slaves to the whites — I had had my fill of their ilk in Jamaica, and they, no doubt of me. Their black chattels, by contrast, seemed at least grateful for my ministrations and accorded me a measure of respect, so lacking in their masters! I came to learn a great deal about these slaves over the years; not least, their herbal remedies and cures, regarding which I have conducted some few experiments and written the occasional paper on 'bush medicine'.

At some later period of this evening I speak of —

I conjectured, in retrospect, it was close to eleven o'clock, as my flagon of rum was quite diminished — a loud knocking interrupted my reverie. The hammering on the door was accompanied by an insistent crying, almost a wail, distinguishable over the noise of the rain and wind:

'Massa Fraser, Maas Fray, Maas Fray!'

On opening the door, I beheld against the cascading heavens, an indeterminable figure enshrouded in a cloak which, once loosened in the shelter of my hallway, revealed Esther, one of the older estate labourers. She had been known to me since my arrival at Refuge, as she was one of Gitten's slaves whom I had first attended — a difficult childbirth, I think it was — and whom I had continued to treat; although since emancipation in 1834, far less frequently, for now that the estate provided neither medical attention nor drugs, she was hard-pressed to afford even my modest fee from her humble wage.

I therefore assumed that this summons, at such an hour and in such inclement weather, must be of an urgent nature and asked:

'Why Esther! What is it? What is the matter, woman?'

'Maas Fraser, for Jesus sake, come quick! Come with me . . . he sick, he sick bad, bad . . . he hardly breathing. I think he time come . . . but not yet, please Lord, not yet . . .'

At this point, she fell to weeping silently, a development which alarmed me greatly. I must explain that I have known Esther to suffer pains, sorrows and griefs (which would have broken a lesser woman) and yet remain intractable, unmoved, maintaining a cold dignity that invited neither sympathy, pity nor enquiries as to her inner state. In my idle moments, I fancied her of the same mould as myself, independent, if not contemptuous of the world and what it offered. With solicitude, then, I endeavoured to soothe her, desiring to discover the meaning of her words:

'Calm yourself, Esther, I pray you. Recover yourself. Who is it that is ill? Is it the boy?'

'Just come, Massa Fraser; please to come and help him. You will see . . .'

I was torn between two responses to her request. I thought of the contrast between my warm, dry abode and the cheerless prospect without. Why should I go abroad at this unsocial hour, when my recompense would be slight, and, no doubt, rheumatism might once again trouble me? No doubt the youth had a bad cold — *all* would be similarly afflicted by the end of these rains, the negroes in their wretched hovels no more than the Gittens females in their well-appointed boudoirs! Yet it also struck me that if Esther was thus reduced to the emotional frailty so common in her sex, then the case must indeed be grave.

Accordingly, without a word more, I fetched my cape, bag and stick, and followed her into the chill and miserable torrent. My surprise at the woman's behaviour was matched by the astonishment I felt at what I subsequently made out through the sheets of rain, to be a dray with two horses standing at the ready! Where in Heaven's name had Esther come by such a thing? Hardly from her fellow negroes, I assumed, for she had long been characterized by estate gossip as a withdrawn, unsocial woman, not given to mixing with the labourers; and I knew for a fact she possessed no such luxury herself. However, enticed by the promise that I "would see", and glad of the respite from an arduous journey on foot, I mounted the cart and we set off through the mud, sans lantern, sans guide, at a pace so reckless it seemed the horses of the Appocalypse drew our vehicle!

The journey from my dwelling to Esther's was scarce two miles; like myself, she had chosen to live far removed from the estate where she toiled. I thought this due to her solitary nature and to the hatred she bore Gittens, who had handed over her husband to the militia after the conflagration of 1816. Why had she stayed here at all, I had wondered? For this land, this "Refuge", can only be the source of disquieting memories for her. Unquiet memories... to counteract the cold rain that lashed my face and trickled down my neck, I refreshed myself from my travelling flask. The warmth of the brandy quickly spread through my veins, as fire, flames through the dried canes, warming my elderly bones.

●

That was what first awakened me all those years ago. The fire. The smell, the sound, the flickering light of acres upon acres of sugar cane blazing out of any control. Plumes and trails of sparks rose heavenward, and as I looked from the windows of my somewhat elevated cottage, befuddled by sleep — for I had retired early after a lavish Easter Sunday repast, accompanied by the fine madeira I had been reserving for the occasion — it seemed as if the entire horizon was aflame, and the sky a gruesome blood-red.

I watched, amazed, for some time, until the bullish roars of Gittens echoed in the distance, summoning the slaves from their quarters and shouting for water! water! Yet the place seemed deserted. Only a handful of domestics turned out in response to his cries, and the dark line of huts where the field slaves resided, remained ominously silent. Deciding at length to venture forth, I discovered from a distracted footman that there was some sort of insurrection afoot; that the bulk of the slaves had quit the plantation for an unknown destination; that the fields of high ripe canes had been put to the torch; and that Massa Gittens was vexed for true!

I witnessed the impotence of the small number of remaining men to quell even the outermost flames of the inferno that had once been cane fields, and on being advised by Gittens that worse was to come, and I had best barricade myself within the great house against roaming savages, I returned to my cottage in disgust. Scenes of overreaction have always filled me with contempt, and I had no intention of sharing the night's vigil with the inmates of Gitten's mansion! Instead, I filled several pails with water from the well, and placed these within my doorway; locked all my lower windows; and arming myself with a musket and a decanter of brandy, settled in an easy chair by my bedroom window to observe what might ensue.

I am ashamed to confess that I was unable to sustain my vigil, and woke, cramped and confined in my chair, early the next morning, my musket at my feet and a scene of smoky desolation before my eyes. It was not until days later that I was given to understand the extent of the 1816 uprising. Apparently, the slaves, restless and angry at what they perceived as the denial of their freedom by the planters (this freedom, they were assured, having been procured by Mr. Wilberforce and their friends in England) had decided to take matters into their own hands, and to fight for what they considered rightfully theirs — Barbados. Led by an African-born negro of Bayley's Estate, one Bussa, and organized by his competent "lieutenant", Jackey, drivers and watchmen and other artesians from plantations throughout the island had met secretly to plan the revolt.

I was acquainted with Bussa by sight only, but he had always seemed to me an impressive figure, coal-black with grey at his temples, and a dignified bearing — I could well believe him and his followers to be the architects of such an heroically foolish undertaking. Fired by the oratory of their leaders, the slaves had determined to take control of their destiny and claimed, according to Colonel Codd, commander of the imperial troops stationed in the island, that Barbados 'belonged to them and not to the whiteman whom they proposed to destroy.'

From what I knew of the said "whiteman" in this part of the Empire, I could not but applaud their reasoning; yet was I myself of that complexion and had not lived these twenty odd years to be slaughtered or roasted by anyone, in a quarrel which was none of mine! For this reason, I remained indoors all that day, uncalled for and content withall. I recall hearing distant musket fire, later becoming louder and then retreating once more — I later heard that the local militia had confronted and dispersed the poorly armed but daring rebels in Christ Church, and that the imperial troops had marched on our parish late in the evening of Easter Monday, April 15, but decided to wait until daybreak to attack. I heard that arson and looting had continued apace throughout the area; but as I myself was untroubled, I enjoyed the holiday not a whit less for the unusual state of events.

That evening, however, my peace was disturbed at last, and what I then passively witnessed, from my darkened window, brought home to me the full import of the rebellion which would change forever the temper of life in our colony. I was alerted first by shouts and cries, drawing nearer, until the entire compound resounded with the cacophony of voices, and the evening sky, still angry with the crimson of flames, revealed hundreds of dusky shapes assembling by the slave quarters.

As far as I could determine from my rather distant post, there was a division within the multitude — the smaller group, I conjectured, was a faction of the reble "army", for they remained somewhat aloof from the mass of the crowd, who moved about the yard with great energy but little direction. There were women and children among this latter group, and much running to-and-fro, with small spots of light pinpointing hurriedly contrived cooking fires. Whether these fires were the inspiration for what followed next I cannot tell, but shortly, the outhouses and estate buildings began to smoke and spark, and finally roared into flame. Undoubtedly alarmed by these developments, Gittens and his party fired shots from the reinforced great house, which served only to attract the mob so that it now turned, with cries of delight, on the target which had previously been ignored.

At this point, I must say that my own fears were awakened. Perhaps for the first time, I realized that this was no quaint festival but rather a drama in which death and destruction were likely to be the chief players! Smoke and floating cane-trash swirled in the air, my eyes watered and my throat constricted; I felt as if I were witnessing a vision of hell itself. By the time the first tongues of flame licked at Gitten's prized dwelling — where I myself had dined and afterwards, replete, smoked at my leisure on the wooden verandah — my musket was loaded at the ready; for I preceived that once the main course was over, and the great house a funeral pyre, myself should be the next diversion.

At that point, a cry of derision rose from the crowd, and I looked to see a ghostly procession of white shadows emerge from the rear of the mansion, first singly and then *en masse,* fleeing towards the darkness of the main road. My lord planter and his entourage, under extreme provocation, had decided to quit the scene of battle since they could not have the victory! And the mob — to this day I wonder at their restraint — the insurrectionists did nought to prevent the exodus. A bray of mocking calls was their only farewell; indeed, the priority of the crowd seemed now to be the building itself, some tossing brands of fire through the shattered windows, while others darted into the crumbling skeleton, presumably to salvage what they could before the inevitable destruction was complete, and the eves and timbers of the planter's wealth crashed to the earth at last.

They never came for me. I flatter myself in thinking that this was due to my personality or my lack of ostentation; rather, the oversight was due to the fact that my very existence was forgotten! After an hour or two of uninterrupted observation, I toasted my survival with an immense bumper of rum — the largest I have ever consumed, and the like of which I hope never again to have the occasion of drinking, as I fear it addled my brains and dulled my clarity of vision. For most of the night passed in a daze; I slept fitfully at my post, and woke to the sound of drumming, to see dark shadows leaping and dancing against an orange sky; to wild singing and shouts, incoherent yet suggesting triumph, ascending to whatever gods presided over such a pagan rout.

One incident alone impressed itself on me. I had woken yet again, and was staring half-slumbering before me, when my confused thoughts lighted on the spy-glass, a telescope I had acquired some years hence from a "buckra Johnny", who had nothing else to offer in payment for my services. Accordingly, I searched it out, lurching against furniture in the darkness and cursing at my clumsiness; yet not quite daring to strike a light, self-preservation being an instinct most conducive to prudence! I adjusted the twin glasses, and at first my gaze encountered only a blur of black faces, and then focused on several familiar to me from my travels in the parish. The majority, to be sure, were strangers; yet all alike reflected an expression of animation, vitality — nay, joy is the only epithet that will suffice! — such that I had rarely encountered on the faces of blacks in this island. They sang lustily, they danced with abandon, they were — how shall I convey my impression? — *possessed* with emotion as I had never dreamed these surly labourers could ever be.

At length, my vision turned upon a dancing woman, encircled by her fellows, moving rapidly to the rhythm of three sweat-drenched drummers. Clad in a loose garment, she moved and leaped with a light sensuality I had never been privvy to witness, for all the weddings and dances I had observed. Her face was unsmiling, yet ecstatic; she was, in short, beautiful to behold, despite the stain of perspiration, the soot and ash besmirching her hair and gown; comely and regal, with her entire attention focused on her partner, a drably-attired fellow who barely moved opposite her, allowing her to lead and dominate the dance, smiling to himself and applauding, with the circle, this woman, his woman ... with a physical shock, I recognized the face of John Proverbs; and the woman, the woman, of course, was Esther!

Deeming it wise to observe no more, though profoundly drawn to the spectacle below, I threw the telescope from me, downed the last of the bottle, and in due course, slipped into a deep slumber.

By the end of the following day, it was all over. The local militia, swelled by the ranks of the black regiment, had slaughtered hundreds — rebel and innocent alike — and taken even more numerous prisoners. Bussa and his men had fallen, leaders of an army whose weapons were pitchforks and sticks for the most part, and no match for the local and imperial troops. There is, for me, little heroism in blood and corpses, and there were plenty of these in the next few days, as the soldiers dealt with insurrectionists in the island, even as far as the parish of St. Lucy, exercising neither temperance nor mercy in their executions, firing at will upon rebel and bystander, guided solely by anger and retribution.

I could not stomach the scene at Refuge Plantation, as the outraged Gittens, accompanied by a squadron of disinterested imperial soldiers, returned to take possession of his lands, determining on the spot which of his slaves (now captured or voluntarily returned) should be sent to their deaths, and which, by virtue of their cringing protestations of loyalty, should live. He, who had run like a cowed dog; he, who had hardly *seen* those whom he now condemned; he now, perhaps divinely inspired, played God with the lives of those who had stood idly by (for, it emerged, the majority were in this category) while a passionate and foolhardy few attempted the impossible!

But I was not surprised; mankind had rarely pleased me with any deviation from the debasing impulses of self-interest and the will to power. Gittens was no better and no worse than his white compatriots of landed station — furious and humiliated, I suspect, at being made fools of by those to whom they hardly accorded the gift of reason; and the insult of these savages' temerity in claiming — as was reiterated over and over to the investigative committee subsequently appointed — that this was *their* land, where their ancestors were buried, and they wanted control of it.

Martial law was not lifted until July 12, by which time the reconstruction of Gitten's estate was well underway — typically, an exact replica of what had existed, prior to the events which the entire Government was bent on wiping from the island's history! Those slaves who had died or been executed, numbering perhaps one thousand, were as ciphers, quickly erased from the memories of those who had been for a short time at their mercy; while the one white and two black militiamen who perished in the fray, were lauded to the skies. For a time, there was talk of Bussa and Jackey, and other leaders such as one Mingo, and also a free mulatto from St. John, named Cain Davis, who had fought so that the children of his enslaved wife might be free. But by September, life resumed its normal course; although the damage to the canes had ruined many a planter, and aggrieved distrust on the faces of the whites, sullenness on those of the blacks, made for an almost palpable atmosphere of tension and unpleasantness wherever I went on my rounds, after resuming my duties.

Esther had been spared; her husband John Proverbs, and many of his fellow slaves who had not died in battle or after, had been incarcerated in Bridgetown, awaiting an unenviable fate, if, as was almost certain, implicated in the abortive revolution.

Now, thirty six years later, here was I, in company with that same Esther; and, as if seeking some trace of that dancer in the face she had worn all these years, I found myself stealing a glimpse at her features through the pelting rain, as we jolted over the rough track to her dwelling. I had witnessed the birth of this woman's child; I had gazed at her transfiguration on the night of the fires; and even now, as I respectfully averted my eyes from her features, carved and aged by grief, I recalled a previous occasion on which I had been startled by the depth of naked emotion revealed on her face.

This last occurred on the afternoon of January — fifteen, I believe, but am not positive — in the year 1817. I had been forced to visit Bridgetown to replenish my medical stock, sorely depleted in the aftermath of the uprising; for all seemed so devastated by the unlikely events that a veritable plethora of minor complaints had necessitated my attentions. Although these were largely due, as far as I could tell, to emotional distress, several elderly whites succumbed to the shock without any hope of recovery, and were eventually buried only weeks after the Easter violence.

On this day in January, as I made my way along the careenage, I witnessed a large crowd, and on approaching nigh, was given to understand that the remainder of the rebels — those who had not met death by torture and execution — were being shipped off the island, banished to a colony of Africa named Sierra Leone, with which I was not familiar. Some one hundred of these manacled fellows, I saw, were being led in a solemn procession, heavily guarded, towards a large vessel christened "Francis and Mary", that stood at the ready. A keen student of human physiognomy even then, I forced my way through the assembled throng in order to examine the faces of those men, condemned to exile.

To my surprise, the vast majority, although obviously weakened by imprisonment, appeared to be without any emotion, moving forward mechanically, their features blank and expressionless. One or two wept, and a few showed signs of trepidation — perhaps they had been told of the horrors of the sea-voyage endured by their forbears *en route* to Barbados. It was chiefly the onlookers' demeanour that suggested the gravity of the situation, for a steady wailing and sobbing arose from the gathered black women and children, a hopeless, keening sound that could not fail to touch the heart.

Scanning this crowd, I espied Esther, her face torn with a mixture of anger and loss. While tears ran down her face, and her mouth worked with sorrow, her eyes remained — as on the previous occasion — fixed upon John Proverbs, one of the prisoners; for his part, he seemed to return her one glance and no more on his silent progress forward to the ship. One glance and no more. And that of such quiet determination, that at the time I thought it contempt, and could not fathom the cause. Once glance from a face so still, so calm, yet uncowed, unbroken — rather, assured of some certainty which perhaps it was beyond poor Esther to comprehend. I have seen such an expression on the faces of men about to die.

Esther withdrew into stolid indifference thereafter. She continued to work the fields, refusing any offer of domestic work in the great house, and lived so much unto herself that one often ceased to notice her existence. All the life of the feelings seemed to have left her — until now — since she bid her man an eternal farewell, there on the quayside.

●

At length we arrived, and I followed Esther into her damp and humble dwelling, glad to be out of the rain and done with these thoughts of the past. The room's interior was dark and smoky from a lamp that was placed by the bed. Nevertheless, I was able to make out her grown son, standing in the shadows, somewhat subdued, but obviously healthy. Who, then, was the figure unmoving upon the bed? As I approached, I perceived an older man — some relative perhaps? — Eyes closed the chest barely moving, the face grizzled, the hair grey, the face . . . the face . . . dear God, the face of John Proverbs! Many years older, to be sure, but the same John Proverbs whom I myself had witnessed departing the island forever!

I hardly recall the next hour, so great was my astonishment. I ascertained the man was fatally afflicted with a fever, undoubtedly exacerbated by water on the lungs, and could not be long for this world. I remember administering certain syrups, and advising his wife of the appropriate treatment, without fully acquainting her of the gravity of his condition. Then I was offered refreshment, and settled at the small table with a flagon of warmed rum, I began to fortify myself for the return journey, my thoughts all a jumble. And it was well I thus collected myself, for a further revelation awaited me!

The door opened and another elderly man, accompanied by a woman, entered and paid their respects. I assumed solicitious neighbours; and after some whispered conversation, Esther approached and introduced them to me as Robert Chapman and his wife Minnie. Still rather befuddled, it was several moments before I could place the name — until I recollected that of course, Chapman was one of the younger rebels from Refuge, involved in some way with the 1816 uprising, and had been with John Proverbs on the forced voyage to Sierra Leone! I was speechless with wonder. Had these two returned from the grave? Had they perhaps never left Barbados, never been exiled in chains? Indeed, I doubted my very memory, and for once this must have expressed itself upon my countenance, for Chapman seated himself opposite, called for a measure himself, and offered to enlighten me — a most welcome suggestion, to which I silently nodded my assent. What follows is but the outline of his tale, one so fantastic that to this day I am still inclined to doubt.

I have represented here, as best I can, Chapman's own unique and flamboyant style of speech; but the night was exceedingly long, and many a cup was drunk before I made for home — these my readers may accept as mitigating circumstances for a narrative that undoubtedly lacks coherence and polish.

●

'Yes indeed, Maas Fraser, I was sick. I sick so bad, I hardly notice the militia men always watching, watching us as if, be Chrise, we was going to run away! Run whey? We was all lock up in one big cabin, and even when we get out to walk above deck, most o' we so sick we could barely stan' up! But all the time these soldiers standing around, guns and sword and all kind of weapon, just eager to sieze we and throw we into that terrible sea! You know, Massa Fray, I often wonder how a man could stand up straight on a ship that always moving dis way -dat way- dis way- dat way . . . I been thinking on this a long time, and I feel it mus' be . . .'

'Don't worry the doctor with all your ideas, Robert Chapman — (Minne scolded) — Tell your story and leh we go home!'

'Well, sir, I can't rightly tell how long we are on this vessel, or which way we going, or whey we stop, but in time we reach to Africa, to Freetown Port . . . in Sierra Leone.

'I don't remember everything, you know sir, not these days. But after we came off the ship, more soldiers to meet us. And more jail. And endless talk about handing we over from this governor to that governor; and how we are forbidden to leave this colony on pain of death; and how we should thank the Almighty for our reprieve, since we are not executed and dead, but here in this worthy land to labour with our bodies, and contemplate our sins; and plenty more, but I don't recall everything. Because afterwards, when we are lock up in the town jail — and I tell you, I praise the Saviour then for solid ground! — afterwards, this missionary priest come and tell us the same thing!

'But he was a kind man, Massa Fray, I mus' be just. In truth, in the next years, we had many dealings with these preachers and missionaries, and only one or two of them, I can say, they were bad men. One of them, God damn him, he was such a wretch that if I had a knife ... But to keep to the history; the place where they build the colony was quite small. And there was plenty black man, from the West Indies, and some who say they come from England also — but it took me many years, many years, before I believe them. For I know, I have *read,* sir, that England is the country of white people, from the Queen at the top right down to the lowest.

'Yet these black men ... and all FREE, I forget to tell you this, all free, every man of us. After all the fighting we do in Barbados to get the freedom those damn planters hiding from us ...'

(Here his voice was lowered and he seemed greatly agitated at memories of the rebellion which obviously over-came him. In time, with the aid of a large draught of rum, he calmed himself and continued). 'So there it was, all these free blackman, and the militia ... when we came, only white soldiers, but after some years, black ones also ... and many, many men of God. In the first weeks we settle down in our quarters, it was they who spoke to us. Telling us that Sierra Leone is a new kind of colony, and all of us are here to show the world what we can do; with hard work and the help of the Lord, we can make a new society; but first we must reject our sinful ways and pray for forgiveness, and put our past life behind us, and much more of this kind of talk...'

'You should have listen to them more, Robert Chapman!' (Minnie again!) 'For it seem you forget those words of wisdom. Look, how much rum you drink here tonight?'

(Chapman ignored the interpolation, and proceeded).

'I can't say they were not good men. No, sir, they were good men. They wanted to end slavery, to make *all* free, and they say plenty folks in England also working for this; but we, now slaves no more, we had to *show* these worthy people what we could do, that we was good Christian men.

'So we worship. Dear Father, we worship three times on Sunday, and every day prayers and sermon! Every day hearing how we must not harden our hearts, forgive as we had been forgiven, and work for Jesus.

'An' when we not praying, we working. Hard work — mostly farming, in the fields and on the hillside; a little sugar, you know, but not like the plantation here — and some coffee, and yam and other things to eat.

'Well, we live near to Freetown... that was the main town, Maas Fraser... it was not so big when we come, but more people arriving on the ships, and also Africans from in the countryside. So the colony getting bigger, and now is trading making money. We didn't grow so much, we trade — we trade with the other African people up and down the coast, and then selling the goods to England, to foreign peoples; many ships going and coming in the harbour. Then Freetown is a lively place, indeed! Many shops, and taverns, people from all over the world, and . . .'

'Yes, yes? And woman! Women and and liquor, isn't that right, Robert? Women and drinking and all the vice of Sodom and Gommorah! White women? Or African woman, with face all mark up and paint up? Massa Fraser, *he* won't tell you, but I swear he had a wife over there! Another wife, against the teachings of Our Lord Jesus Christ! African wife, maybe *plenty* wife and pickney too...'

'I not talking 'bout no woman or no chile, Mistress Chapman, so be still! I am here telling the doctor about the times in which I lived, and the trading which was use to make the colony very prosperous after we were there a long time'

(He hurried on, anxious to avoid what appeared to be a contentious point with his wife. I aided him in this, by enquiring whether he and his compatriots had not also been 'prosperous'?)

'Rich, sir? On the little moneys we get for payment? Rich! *We* was not in trade, I beg your pardon if I led you wrongways, the ones who got rich was the *educated* people, the government people . . . although there was black men in the government also, who could speak as beautiful as a bishop!

'No, we work as farmers, most of us. Also, sometimes in building — roads and barn and house, all manner of constructions. And with all this building and worshipping and learning, what time we could have for woman and chile, I ask you? No time at all!

'Yes sir, we had lessons too, with the missionaries, to learn the scriptures and, for those who

33

could not read, to learn that also, as well as writing, figures, and information from chap-books which the society sent from England. John also use to read the newspapers, and he would tell us what they said . . .'

(At these words, our thoughts returned to the silent figure recumbent upon the simple bed; and to the brooding woman at his side, wiping his brow with damp cloths as I had instructed, her gaze fixed on his face, waiting, perhaps, for his eyes to open, for him to speak her name. One glance and that was all.

The atmosphere within the smoke-filled hut changed perceptibly. Even Chapman's visage altered, and grew more pained and solemn, as if remembering the years of strangeness, of isolation from loved ones and familiar sights; and of the loneliness of the Barbadians in the midst of negroes with whom they shared little beyond the colour of their skin and the rudiments of language. Chapman grew passionate on this matter of distinctions).

'Of course we did not friend with all, regardless! We are from Barbados! What did we have in common with those of Jamaica, or England, or the Americas? What do we know, eh, what do we know of their ways? Not because we are all once from Africa, Massa Fraser, that white people think we all the same! I assure you, sir, while I was in that land of my exile, I met a great number of Africans from many parts of that land, who knew nothing of each other; far less of *my* country! What do strange negroes know of us, I ask? What we eat; how we dance; our days of festival — all our customs; none of them have buried their navel-string here in Barbados! None of them have buried their mother and grandmother here on this land. How then, sir, how, I am asking you, could we all be the same?'

(To this I answered not, for certainly the question was rhetorical).

'No, fuh sure. We kept together, those of us from Barbados. Well, most of us . . . some of the *younger* fellows became . . . became 'intimate' with women of African tribes. They learned the African languages. They slowly left our company . . . but *we* remained loyal to our homeland, yes.

'John would read to us from the newspapers, any news of Barbados. We look, oh Lord, we look . . . every time there is names of the dead, or slaves the governor hang, or that get sold to another estate . . . we look, until eye-water comes, to see if anybody we know is written there. I don't know if it was more pain to see the name, or not to see it; because when the name is not there, anything could have happen — sickness, another child — another child that belong to another wufless man!

'But these things we never talk about; we only speak of the old days, and of the battles and the fires and the dancing, Lord, the sweet night before the militia kill Bussa and Jackey and all those brave, brave warriors . . . and take us, and lock us up . . .

'John read the newspapers and tell us, even before the missionaries tell us, that slavery days ending. Freedom time for Barbados come at last! Eighteen hundred and thirty four, Lord bless the time . . . we drink the night we hear, Minnie, we drink and consider about all our kin at home drinking too, an' dancin', and the drums, bam ba bam bam! bam ba bam bam! And those days, we feel like young lads again. We still working, praising God, we learning, we doing everything the same way but we thinkin', well if massa day done, we free in Barbados jus' like we free in Sierra Leone!

'And we really free now in Sierra Leone, meaning, you see, that now we could leave the place if we did want, we no longer bound to stay! For that was another burden over there — we was free but we couldn't go and come as we please. I did really wish to travel when I was there, you know... to see some of the place I hear my great granny tell of, maybe even find someone who hear about my family far away in Barbados... but no way I could try! We was free, yes, but we bound to stay in the colony on pain of death! What kind of freedom that? At least back home we use to go from here clear over St. Michael to somebody wake, or visit a sweetheart... It was that way, Massa Fray, I first meet Minnie. She use to work over by the estate where they had a big windmill, the one they call...'

'Leave me out, Robert! The doctor not interested in how you court me. And dear God only knows, this here is not the place to talk of loving, when poor John so sick.'

'Yes, Minnie, very well, you are right. Well John... John read all he could find out, and he tell us about this thing they call 'apprenticeship'. Where all the slave in Barbados free, but they can't move neither. They free, but they still mus' work the plantation, and the little wages they getting can't pay for all the things Massa Gittens stop give them — clothing, food, even now they have to pay rent! Rent, you can imagine, for this where hog wouldn't live! Free? They wasn't free at all, we figure. Was more lie and deceit like these damn, gor-blame planters always practicing on black people! If I was here that time, I would have ...

'Anyway, we feel so sorrowful when we get to

see what was really happening. One ole fellow, he use to drink a lot of the African wine, and then he use to plan and plan how he going home, and what a festivity they would have for him, and all his grandchildren would come to sit on his knees, how he would bring them all the money he save up — for all of we save hard, Massa Fray, every week we putting aside a little for the time when . . . Well, when this ole fellow understand that is not real freedom yet, nothing really change in Barbados, he go into Freetown and he drunk so bad he never wake up, just mumbling and weeping, bawling in he sleep, bawling for he wife, he pickney, bawling for Barbados that he never see again.

'After he die, John get hard. He bide his time, and he spend many hours with the missionaries; then he tell us that full freedom *going* to come, *must* come; and sure enough, praise Jesus, as all here present must forever celebrate in their hearts, Barbados slave FREE on firs' a August, eighteen thirty eight! And as I hear, then is when festival start in the lan'!

'This time, we didn't think and dance. We sit down at night, an' we plan. We plan how we going home. One say we could run way and don't ask nobody, go down the coast and try to steal a boat. Another think we must go and beg the governor to repatriate us to our native island of our birth. And a next fellow say we must write to the governor of Barbados, because maybe he wouldn't remember the trouble in 1816, it was so long ago. Every week we having meeting; we reading the newspapers to see how everything is being arrange; we saving our wages to buy passage on a ship. But you know how when a lot of people coming together for a purpose, everyone have a different plan to make it happen?

That was us, sir — those men could never reach any agreement.

'Well, John was acquainted with a teacher, a black man from England, and him, John and your humble servant, myself, we had a lot of consultations together and finally we decide to write a letter. A letter to the Queen of England, Victoria of Great Britain! John write the letter; to tell the truth, I don' know how many times John Proverbs write that letter! Every time he show it to the teacher or the other men, something else to go into it, something have to change or write in a more educated manner. But finally, it was finish, and spell out on good paper with the best ink we could buy. And he send it by a parson who was going to England, and we who had a clear hand sign our name, for us and for the rest also. We ask the Queen to let us go home.

'And she write back — after a long time, she write back . . . well, some one of her people write back, to tell us we can't go home but we could go to Jamaica, because they were looking for Africans to work on the plantations there as indenture servants! Can you imagine this, Maas Fray? We want to go home and they tell us to go to Jamaica!

'Well, it only take a month this time for us to write the answer, we were so vexed. This time we say . . . but you could read it yourself, doctor! Only this one is not so elegant like the one we sent, this only a copy I make myself.'

(At this juncture, Chapman drew from his waistcoat pocket an obviously treasured parchment, creased and frayed but still legible to my eyes, once I had located my spectacles. By his permission, I reproduce the letter verbatim below):

*To Her Most Gracious Majesty
Victoria, Queen of the United
Kingdom of Great Britain
and Ireland, Defender of the Faith.*

*Sierra Leone
13th May, 1841.*

The Humble Memorial of your Majesty's most dutiful Barbadian Subjects being inhabitants of the colony of Sierra Leone:-

That your Memorialists have learned with deepest satisfaction that your Most Gracious Majesty has asked whether your Memorialists feel a desire to emigrate to Jamaica, one of your Majesty's West India Islands.

Your Memorialists having taken into consideration your Majesty's Royal wish, begs most respectfully to say that, notwithstanding your Memorialists duly appreciate the kind mark and condescension shown by your Majesty, yet your Memorialists cannot but feel it their bounden duty to express with extreme sorry and regret that as the boon is not held out by your Most Gracious Majesty by which your Memorialists can return back to their own native island, they decline going to the Island of Jamaica in consequence of your Memorialists being totally ignorant of the manner and customs of that place.

In conclusion, your Memorialists most respectfully crave that should your

Most Gracious Majesty be pleased to grant that your Memorialists be allowed to return back to Barbados, the place of our nativity, your Memorialists will feel extremely grateful for the same, and by which your Memorialists will endeavour to avail themselves of doing so without causing any immediate expense to your Majesty, and thus by that means it will save your Majesty from any further trouble for our transportation from this colony to any of your Majesty's West Indian Islands . . .

> John Proverbs
> John Morgan
> Robert Chapman
> J. Thomas

Acting for and on behalf of the other Barbadian subjects who have agreed to the foregoing statement'.

(According to Chapman, the Governor of Sierra Leone was subsequently asked to supply Her Majesty's Government in Britain with an evaluation of the characters of the Barbadian petitioners. From sources within the Sierra Leone administration, they learned that this Governor had recommended the men as obviously reformed (thanks to the influence of the colony), faultless in behaviour, and as being harmless old men wishing only to return to their "native island" for burial. He was even so good as to forward another letter from the applicants, which had been submitted to him by the teacher, earlier mentioned, for approval.

I had the good fortune to trace the correspondence recently, if only to prove to myself that this fantastic interchange of letters was based on fact. My copy of the aforementioned letter follows).

Sierra Leone
5th July, 1841

The Right Honourable
Lord John Russell.

My Lord,

I have the honor to transmit to your Lordship a Memorial addressed to her Most Gracious Majesty from the Barbadians deported to this Colony in the year 1819. Their object is to obtain the sanction of Her Majesty's Government to return to their native island Barbados. They seem to have no desire to emigrate to any other Colony. I owe it, however, to them to state to your Lordship that I have always found them an orderly and well conducted body of individuals. I would therefore beg to recommend their case to your Lordship's favourable consideration.

I have the honor to be

Most respectfull my Lord
Your Lordship's Most Obedient and
Most Humble Servant

John Carr
Acting Governor.

'Well sir, Massa Fray, you see me here, and so you know that after our time of tribulation in foreign lands, we were granted release, like the children of Israel. All those months we waited to hear the Queen's answer, John hardly spoke, except to his acquaintance in the governor's office, who was familiar with the mail. Every day, the governor get letters. You know how much letters a governor get? The amount of paper must weigh down the ship what bring it, Lord! And every day, we passing by after work, to see John face — not like we looking, you understand, we just passing by as if we barely notice him; but we could see on John face that the answer don't come. I recall some nights, we drink all night, only for to make us sleep and not mind the waiting too much.

'But the day come. It was the thirtieth of September, 1841 — I know the date in my heart, as good as my own birthday, which, to be truthful, I am not *exactly* positive about... but I remember, to the hour, the day that Minnie and I get married by Parson Beacon — you remember it, Minnie? In fact, you remember it better than me ... But as I was telling you, Maas Fray, on that date, the letter came, and we could *see* the news on John's blessed face, God bless him, Lord, God bless my brother and spare him Jesus, spare this man, my friend and true countryman ...'

(Chapman covered his face, overcome with emotion. I felt he was remembering the jubilation at the long-awaited news, reliving its effect upon his dear friend and compatriot, moved to tears of joy at the gladness that letter brought them all; and he was racked with sorrow at the mortal change wrought by time on that same friend, the contrast between John Proverb's face now, and on receipt of the good tidings those many years ago.

To avoid discomfitting the man, and to cover the awkward silence, I took from the table the facsimile of that fateful letter which he had produced with shaking fingers during the narrative; once more, I set down exactly what I read).

Colonial Office
30th September 1841

John Carr Esq., or
the Officer administering the
Government of Sierra

Sir,

I have to acknowledge the receipt of your dispatch No. 14 of the 5th of July with the memorial therein enclosed addressed to the (Office) by certain persons natives of Barbadoes, who pray that they may be allowed to return to that Island from whence they were deported in the year 1816 and I have to desire that you acquaint the memorialists that Her Majesty's Government have no objection to their removing themselves to Barbados.

RT. Honourable
John Russell.

(When I had ceased to examine this startling evidence, I looked up, and observed poor Chapman yet distraught. However, to my surprise, Minnie took up the tale, and began to relate the events consequent on the Secretary's formal release of them from exile).

'It was over a year from then, sir, Esther get a letter from John Proverbs. To this day, we don't know how it finally reach, it take so long to come. She could hardly read it, she so frighten! Well, John tell she that he trying to come home, and also Robert, and the other John, and some of the men who went on the same ship. How they not coming home as slaves, nor coming home to be slaves, but they were coming home as free men in the law, soon as they could manage; they were coming home to us. . .

(Here Minnie glanced in Esther's direction as if for confirmation; but the latter remained fixed at her post, apparently unhearing, a woman from whom all feeling had gone, a well dry of moisture, still as marble. I longed to hear of the women's reaction to such earth-shattering news, but Chapman, having recovered himself, began to explain).

'You see, Maas Fray, it was not so easy. Plenty form to fill out. All kind of document to sign. Then to seek a ship going our way; most only travelling to England, and we didn't have enough money for a roundabout route. And then again, there was a younger fellow, Jimmy — he was sickly, he hadn't manage to save all his passage. Some of the men wanted to go and leave him, but most of we reckon that since we get on the "Francis and Mary" together, well, we not going home one-one! We leaving Sierra Leone together.

So we labour on, saving the pennies and making enquiries, until after a long time we find a ship that would take us for the money we had. But then I got sick . . . I got the dysentry, and I couldn't travel . . . and John *made* them wait for me, he had them hold on another while . . . until at last, after so many years — not bad years, sir, not *bad* years, but years and years away from where our life began;

after all these years we go on board a steamship, a blasted mail-ship, stopping everywhere up and down the coast for passenger and post; finally, praise God, we go out into the deep water, leaving Africa behind only a kind of dark green shadow on the edge of the world, farewell, farewell and *we* going home! Lord we going home.

'There were plenty Africans on the ship, bound for Jamaica to work their indenture, so we were a large number; no chains this time, although the space we had to live was small like a gaol! But we could go up and down as we please, providing we don't go in the white people's part. And since there were plenty missionaries and religious there, they talk to us and some share their food, so we wasn't too uncomfortable.

'I shame to say, but I was sick again. Most of the time sick — I swear then an oath to Christ, I never gone go 'pon the sea again, not even a fishing boat! — and I didn't know much of what happening. But I hear since that the men quiet, quiet and thinking, contemplating on all that had passed — before we left Barbados, and ever since. Thinking of our plans and our fighting, of Bussa and Jackey and Cain Davis and Mingo and all the others. Thinking that if we never fight, we could have never leave children and land, never been alone, outcast, like the damned souls in the Bible.

'But you know, when I ask them later on, not one of them say he was sorry he fight. Not one of them say he wouldn't do it again if he have to — only this time, he would do it better!

'You going to think, Maas Fraser, that we land in Barbados with pomp an' ceremony. But I here to tell you, not so at all! We come off the ship with the Africans, who stopping here before Jamaica, and we feel strangers just like them. No wife, no child to meet we. No one at all. That is when a man could break, I tell you. You see your land, you see the beaches, and the town and the careenage getting closer and closer. You can see the men on the quay, pulling rope and throwing rope. But you don't see you kinfolk. And all the feelings in you heart dying, getting small-small, and you think, "They never get the letter, they don't even know I coming!" or worse: "They get the letter, but they don't want to come — they shame; or dead; or have a new man.."

'And then you see the soldiers coming and you think, "Dear Jesus, all these years and all these miles and they coming to lock up my arse again? What the hell mek me try this foolishness to come home? I old and stupid for sure — I mad in truth!"

'But they only hold us a short time. To tell us, be quiet. Not to make a big celebration. We must be very careful. They *always* watching us. They don't forget us. We must live very peaceful. And now, register with the Colonial Secretary — yes, he know we were coming, he know *all* about us; and now you can go, but remember . . .

'Remember? Remember? All we could do is to remember. As we walking from the wharf, all of we quiet like mouse, we remember how we went on another ship, what? Thirty or more years past? Remembering who was there to see us leave, and where they are now? Remembering why it was we had to go, the terror of those times but the glory also, oh yes Lord, the glory! Remembering what the town did look like then, and noticing how it change here, and the road get wider there, and look! The new shops! And the clothes those girls wearing!

'That day, we walked for miles. Until the different men get their courage and went for transport to their own places. One here saying goodbye; another afraid to leave, to find what waiting at home. Until is just me, John Proverbs and two others, get a trap to St. Philip. And before we get to Refuge Plantation, no one saying a word to the other, we stop the driver and pay him, and we walk the last mile to the estate.

'But before we reach the boundary, we see the black people — not in the road, but to the side, in the field, like they working, but all the time looking up, looking up the road until as they see us, one by one they stop, and slow like duppy they coming to the roadside, standing, staring, waiting. So we go up to them.

'Oh God forgive me, doctor, but you can't know the terror in a man heart as he looking, searching with he old eye, eye full up o' water, 'fraid to death he won't see who he wanting to see. Fraid he come all this way, leave what he know, what he use to, leave all he friends, and come back to strangers, to die here alone, alone. I so frighten in the middle of all them duppy man an' woman, I nearly piss myself! I look to John but he just take one glance and find Esther. (One glance and that was all). But me, me alone, and I start to shake, until — I feel a chile pull my shirt an' ask if is true I am she grandpa, an' I look up and see Minnie, and my son (how he big! Lord — a big, big man now, but I know is Seth) and baby Ruth, with pickney in she arms (I wonder is for which man? And I hope she married he!) and then Minnie, Minnie come to me and she say, "Robert Chapman, you come home, man, you come back to we. You come back to Barbados".'

●

The returned rebels led, as instructed, a quiet life. Too old for labour, they used their savings and the earnings of their families, to live simply (and piously) for the few years remaining to them. Yet on a small plantation, and among those nearby, history lives — at night, in hushed conversations, in songs and tales of the slaves and the freed slaves, the story of Bussa's rebellion and the heroes who had died or been exiled, was told over and over; exaggerated, elaborated, criticized, praised.

The stories lived on, fragmented perhaps, but surviving, especially in the night-time world of those who had no life by day, except as beasts of burden. Those who, free now, had nothing to celebrate, nothing, that is, but heroes long dead and gone — so long ago, that it seemed to the young men and women to be only nancy stories, tales of old mothers and grannies which had no truth for them now.

Yet when these old men began to surface, slowly and silently, in villages and estates throughout Barbados, the stories once more circulated. And in time, the young people crept nearer, spying to see if *that* was the rebel who had led an army against the militia? If *he* was the man they said had been over thousands of miles to Africa and had won the right to come home? From looking on, they approached, they asked their questions, they listened, and they learned.

Times were hard, and the planters of the old days who remained could not afford to notice the breath of life which swept through the 'niggeryard'. Old and decrepit themselves, they never questioned the occasional face glimpsed in the distance, that struck a chord of memory, that brought back vague but unpleasant sensations. They told themselves it was due to age.

And their heirs thought that young John's aged father — or was it his grandfather? — was only a doddering old black, as faceless as Esther, who had long blended into the landscape as far as they were concerned.

But history lives. Don't mek nobody fool you. So it was that a field in Vineyard Plantation, St. Philip, is still called 'Bussa's Field'. And that a village in St. George is named after Mingo. And that, in the same year that John Proverbs died... a rebel, a warrior, a faithful husband, a traveller to distant continents, a patriot who had never ceased his efforts to come home to Barbados ... in the same year as John Proverbs died, in 1850, an adult male in the parish of St. Philip had himself baptized "Cain Davis".

Appendix 1.

The Confession of Robert, a Slave belonging to the Plantation called "Simmons"

Who saith, that some time the last year, he heard the negroes were all to be freed on New-year's Day. That Nanny Grig a negro woman at *Simmons'*, who said she could read, was the first person who told the negroes at *Simmons'* so; and she said she had read it in the Newspapers, and that her Master was very uneasy at it: that she was always talking about it to the negroes, and told them that they were all damned fools to work, for that she would not, as freedom they were sure to get. That, about a fortnight after New-year's Day, she said the negroes were to be freed on Easter-Monday, and the only way to get it was to fight for it, otherwise they would not get it; and the way they were to do, was to set fire, as that was the way they did in Saint Domingo. Further saith, that Jackey, the Driver at *Simmons'*, said he would send to the other Drivers and Rangers, and to the head Carters about, and to bussoe (at *Bayley's*), to turn out on Easter Monday to give the Country a light, and let every body know what it was for; and that John (at *Simmons'*) was the person who carried the summons from Jackey: that Jackey was one of the head men of the Insurrection, and that he had heard him say he was going to point out a good great house to live in, but he did not say which: that Jackey sent also to a free man in *The Thicket* (who could read and write), to let the negroes at *The Thicket* know, that they might give their assistance. That he does not recollect the man's name, but if he saw him, he should know him: that he lives about *The River* Estate, and was a *Simmons'*, with Jackey, two Sundays before Easter.—Further saith, that Mingo, at *Byde-Mill* (the Ranger), came to *Simmons'* on Sunday before Easter: that he saw him go to Jackey's house; and that, in passing the said Jackey's house, he heard Mingo say, that on Sunday night next they were to turn out and give the Country a light, and the Country would be as sure to him as the coat on his back. That he heard Jackey say, that Washington Francklin was to be Governvor, and to live at *Pilgrim.* Jackey used to go very often (sometimes at night) to see Washington Francklin: that he has heard Jackey tell Will Nightingale (who was Jackey's brother-in-law, and belongs to Mrs. Nightingale,) to go to Washington Francklin, and he would tell him what was to be done. That the reason he came to hear these things, was, because Jackey's children were fond of him, and he was in the habit of going to Jackey's house and playing with his children, when the conversations mentioned passed. —He further saith, that on Easter Day, Jackey (at *Simmons'*) told Mingo to go about and pick up all the men, and muster them up at his house, and he would tell them what to do. That Mingo accordingly mustered up the men, and gave all names, and told them they were to meet Judge Gittens' men below his garden. That in the evening, when the whip snapped, all *Simmons'* people came out to know what it snapped for; and after they came as far as the watermill, Jackey told them what it was for. That Jackey, Mingo, and John Baynes, went towards Judge Gittens', and shortly afterwards two fields of canes in that direction were set on fire.—He further saith, that King William (of *Sunberry*) came to *Simmons'* Estate on Monday forenoon (with a red coat and gun) with a gang, and said, "I see nothing in the Manager's house—you, *Simmons'* people, must have taken every thing out; if had not, we would not trouble the buildings:" and then gave orders to break up and burn; and gave orders to William Green, of *Congo Road,* to set fire to the trash heap. That Prince William, of *The Grove* (Mr. Hunt's), came also on Monday aforenoon, on horse-back, with the gang, with a sword in his hand, holding it upright over the horse's head, and gave orders to lick down the sick-house, and also to burn the firld of to lick down the sick-house, and also to burn the field of canes above the sick-house; and rode about the yard, and ordered that mill to be put in the wind. That Toby, of *The Chapel,* came with a gun in his hand, and gave orders to shoot, every one that did not join them, and marched about the yard with a gun on his shoulder. That little Sambo, belonging to *The Adventure,* came with the gang to *Simmons',* armed with a sword, and began to lick down the old mill door, in which they kept the provisions. That Jack; belonging to Mr. Doughty, had a sword and a long knife in his hands, and came up to him (Robert) and said, "I will chop you down if you do not join us."—That Thomas, from *Congo Road,* came with the gang of rebels on Monday forenoon, and was the first that began to chop at the boiling-house door, with a hatchet; and ordered Mingo (belonging to *Congo Road*) to take charge of a box of carpenters' tools which was in the boiling-house. That a man called Charles, belonging to *Sandford's,* was on horseback with the gang, and rode about the yard giving orders. That Thomas, belonging to Mr. Carter, came armed with a sword, and was the first to lick down the door of the sick-house.

Appendix 2.

Slaves From the Island of Barbadoes

The next considerable accession to the population of the colony (independent of the liberated Africans,) was that made in 1819, by the importation of 85 slaves who had been implicated in the insurrectionary movement that occurred amongst the negroes in the island of Barbadoes. The circumstances under which they were received into the settlement, rendered it necessary to retain them for a time under some restrictions, and they appear consequently to have been employed in public works between two and three years after their arrival. At the expiration of this time they were permitted to employ themselves for their own benefit; and their conduct since has proved that this lenity was not ill judged, for since the restrictions were removed they have in general shown themselves to be industrious and useful.

No documents have been kept from which information could be obtained respecting the influence of the climate upon them; it has been therefore found necessary on this subject to inquire of the negroes themselves, more particularly of Samuel Lane, an intelligent man, whose statement will be found in the Appendix (B.) No.8. It will be seen that this statement accounts (though not so satisfactorily as might be wished,) for 60 of the original number. Of these 60, 34 are know to be living, and 26 supposed to be dead. Whether the remaining 25 or any part of them have left the colony, or still remain in it, seems uncertain; amd as they have never been distinctly specified in the census, there are no means of ascertaining the fact.

It is understood that after their dismissal from the public works, the great majority of them settled in or about Freetown. Many being tradesmen readily found employment, and those who had a knowledge of tropical agriculture have latterly been sought after by merchants and other individuals, who have small farms or gardens for their amusement in the vicinity. In some of these the Barbadoes negroes have a few liberated Africans undre their instruction, and thus occupied for their own benefit, render themselves really useful to the colony.

Those of their number who have been conversed with, seemed generally to be contented with their condition, particularly the labouring class; but there was by no means that *decided* expression of satisfaction which perhaps many would have expected from the change in their circumstances.

Appendix 3.
Statement of Samuel Lane Taken March 6th 1826

With respect to himself *Samuel Lane* states that he is a Wheelright by trade — that he came from Barbadoes accompanied by about eighty-seven others, and arrived in the Colony in 1817 or 1818.

Of this number Two went to the Isle de Los, where they died. Four went to York. Two of the four died — the other Two continue to live there.

Three went to the Gambia. Two returned to Sierra Leone, the other remained. The bulk of the Barbadians are in or about Freetown — he believes (sic) about twenty-six have died out of the original number.

On their arrival in this Colony the greater part of them were employed on Government Works for the first three years at the expiration of which, they were discharged by Governr McCarthy.

He believes that those People so discharged are now gaining a livelihood in the Colony, but not a very good one, some by their Trades, and others who have no Trades as Labourers on different little Farms, or as Servants on different Farms, or as Servants when they they can procure employ. Some of the Labourers gain One Pound per month, others who are Headmen and understand planting gain One Pound and Ten Shillings per month

Samuel Lane is employed by Mr. George (an American settler) and receives Thirty Shillings per month, which place he is about to quit because he finds that he cannot maintain himself and Wife on that hire, it will not even find Shoes to their feet. He is now offered employment by Mr. Crews to build a House.

The Carpenters at present employed by Government receive Two Shillings and sixpence per day — which he considers barely sufficient to find a family in food without leaving for cloths (sic) etc.

He is of the opinion that those Barbadians who are at present in the Colony would prefer remaining here as Freemen to returning to Barbadoes to be in Slavery.

Those who had Masters that were cruel and whipped them, are better off here — but those who had kind owners were better off in Barbadoes as Slaves.

Samuel Lane was in happier circumstances there than here. He is of opinion there are more bad Masters than good ones.

With respect to the others with those circumstances he is acquainted Samuel Lane states as follows:

Jacob Thomas is by Trade a Farmer — has a wife and one Child has a lot of land, and a very good Shingle House upon it, keeps a Grog Shop, is in very good circumstances.

Edmund Brathwaite (has a Wife) lives with Mrs. Parker in Freetown as Shopman — has a lot of Land in Maroon Town, and a Shingle House upon it — is a Carpenter by Trade, but does not follow it.

James Giddins — Carpenter by Trade, has a Wife and two Children — has a lot of Land in the grass field, and a Shingle House upon it he works at his Trade sometimes he gets work sometimes not. When he works he gains Three Shillings per day if he would take Two Shillings 6d per day, he might always get work.

Richard Sergeant (Taylor) is Married lives in Freetown — his Wife has a lot and a House upon it and is going well.

Billy Stows (Carpenter) lives at York.

John Probert — Servant to the late Governor, (a Wife and one child) has a lot and a Grass House.

John Robert Carpenter (Wife and Two Children) Lives in Gloster — comes to Freetown to get work as there is no work in the Mountains, is usually employed at Three Shillings or Two (?)s per day.

John Henry Burrows Is a Cook *and a very fine one* (has a Wife and Child) Lives with Mr. Atkins and gains $3 per month, Has a lot and Shingle House in the grass field.

Barrington — a Taylor, is married — has a lot and Boarded House in the grass field — gets but little employ.

Monsieur Barrow, a Servant has a Wife and two Children, also a lot and Boarded House in the grass field Is in bad circumstances.

Cain Davis (Taylor) is Married — has a lot and Shingle House in Maroon Town, a good Workman, with plenty of employ.

John Trial — Servant (is single) has a lot and a Grass House in the grass field. Lives with Mr. Crews gains Thirty Shillings per month

Roche — Labourer (has a Wife and two Children) Superintends a farm for Mr. Weston — his Wife has a lot and Grass House in Freetown, gains Thirty-five Shillings per month and his food.

Samuel Minge, Labourer (Single Man) superintends a Farm for Mr. Clarkston gains Thirty Shillings per month and his food.

Simon Pridie Mason (Single) has a lot and Grass House in Freetown, is a good Workman, has constant employ gains Four Shillings per day.

John Andrew, Labourer (Single) has no house, lives anywhere

Mundy — Labourer (Single) gains nearly nothing.

Hamlet Labourer (Single) gains Fifteen Shillings per month and his food.

William Coopers — Trade a Cooper (Married) has a lot and Boarded House in grass field — is a good Tradesman and gains a good livelihood.

Christopher More — Cooper (Married) has a lot and a House in building on the grass field, is in good employ.

Castilla — Cooper (Single) has a lot and Boarded House in the grass field — gains $4 per month.

Dicky — Cooper (Two children) has a lot and Grass House in the grass field gains Fifteen Shillings per week.

John Andrews — Labourer (Single) is very sickly — has a Grass House.

William Andrews — Labourer (Single) lives with his Brother John.

Samy — Carpenter (Married) lives at Charlotte Town.

Drummers Chief Mason (Single) lately arrived from the Gambia gains Three Shillings per day.

A. Goodin — Labourer (Single) has a lot and a

Grass House in grass field — Superintends Mr. Barbers Farm, gains Thirty Shillings per month and food.

William Lord — Groom (Married) has a lot and a Grass House in a grass field — lives with Mrs. Maccauley gains a great deal of Money — is better off than any one of the Barbadians.

John Richard Labourer (Single) Superintends Mr. Crews' Farm — gains Thirty Shillings per month and food.

Roger Sandford Labourer (Single) Lot and Grass House on grass field, Superintends Mrs. Smith's Farm gains Thirty Shillings per month and his food.

Some Liberated Africans work under those different Superintendants — Lane has one under him, who is a very good workman, and gains Fifteen Shillings per month and his food.

John Morgan, Carpenter (a Wife) lives in Freetown — his Wife has a lot and Shingle House — a good Tradesman, he is seldom out of employ, gains Four Shillings per day.

William Robertson (Shoemaker) (a Wife no child) lives in the grass field at Freetown has a lot and Shingle House upon it consider him very well circumstanced.

Jacky — Labourer (Single) Lot and Grass House in grass field, Superintendant upon Mr. Barbers farm, gains Thirty Shillings per month and food.

Prince William — Groom (Wife had two Children both dead) Lot and Grass House in grass field — lives with Mr. Maccauley gains a great deal of money — better off than any one of the Barbadians.

Appendix 4.

REF/ CO 267/164
P.R.O. London.

To Her Most Gracious Majesty
Victoria Queen of the United
Kingdom of Great Britain and
Ireland, Defender of the Faith

The Humble Memorial of Your Majesty's most
dutiful Barbadian Subjects being Inhabitants of the
Colony of Sierra Leone —

Most Respectfully Shewath
that Ye Memoralists have
learned with deepest satisfaction, that Your
Most Gracious Majesty has been pleased to convey
through Doctor R. R. Madden, Your Royal wish,
whether Your Memorialists feels a desire to Emigrate
to Jamaica, one of Your Majesty's West India
Islands —

Your Memorialists having taken
into consideration Your Majesty's Royal wish, begs
most respectfully to say, that notwithstanding

Your Memorialists duly appreciate the kind mark and condescension shown by Your Majesty yet Your Memorialists cannot but feel it their bounden duty to express with extreme sorrow and regret, that as the boon is not held out by Your Most Gracious Majesty by which Your Memorialists can return back to their own native Island, they decline going to the Island

In conclusion Your Memorialists most respectfully crave, that should Your Most Gracious Majesty be pleased to grant, that Your Memorialists be allowed to return back to Barbadoes, the place of our Nativity, Your Memorialists will feel extremely grateful for the same, and by which Your Memorialists will endeavour to avail themselves of doing so without causing any immediate expense to Your Majesty.

May you and your Royal Regner[long]tlive so rule
the British Empire.

      John Proverbs

      Jhn Morgan

      Robert Chapman

      J. Thomas

Acting for and on the behalf of the other Barbadians
Subjects who have agreed to the foregoing statements

Sierra Leone,
13th May, 1841.

Some Books Published by Karia Press

Available through Bookshops or direct from Karia Press, BCM Karia, London, WC1N 3XX, United Kingdom. Tel: (01)-**249 4446**

For direct orders, enclose payment with order. (Also add handling charge of 15% UK; 20% Overseas)

Short Stories/ Prose Fiction

Song For Simone
and other stories

by Jacob Ross

ISBN 0 946918 29 5 Pb £3.95
ISBN 0 946918 33 3 Hb £8.95

The Day Sharon Lost Her Way Home

by Jennifer Martin
Illustrated by Paul Dash

ISBN 0 946918 23 6 Pb £3.95
ISBN 0 946918 24 4 Hb £5.95

The Earliest Patriots:
Being the true adventures of certain survivors of 'Bussa's Rebellion' (1816), in the island of Barbados and Abroad

by Evelyn O'Callaghan

ISBN 0 946918 53 8 Pb £2.95

Afrikan Lullaby
Folk Tales From Zimbabwe

by Chisiya

ISBN 0 946918 45 7 Pb £1.95

Biography/ Autobiography

The Autobiography of A Zimbabwean Woman

by Sekai Nzenza

ISBN 0 946918 21 X Pb £4.95
ISBN 0 946918 22 8 Hb £8.95

Dispossessed Daughter of Africa

by Carol Trill

ISBN 0 946918 42 2 Pb £4.95
ISBN 0 946918 42 0 Hb £8.95

In Troubled Waters
Memoirs of my Seventy Years in England

by Ernest Marke

ISBN 0 946918 2 5 Pb £4.95

"I Think of My Mother"
Notes on the Life and Times of Claudia Jones

by Buzz Johnson

ISBN 0 946918 02 3 Pb £3.95
ISBN 0 946918 05 8 Hb £8.95

This list represents some books already in print and those soon to be published. For a full list of published and forthcoming publications please write to the address above.

Black People in Britain

We Are Our Own Educators!
Josina Machel: From Supplementary to Black Complementary School

by Valentino A. Jones

ISBN 0 946918 37 6 Pb £3.95

Telling The Truth
The Life and Times of the British Honduran Forestry Unit in Scotland (1941-44)

by Amos Ford

ISBN 0 946918 01 5 Pb £2.95
ISBN 0 946918 03 1 Hb £7.95

Many Struggles
West-Indian Workers and Service Personnel in Britain 1939-45

by Marika Sherwood

ISBN 0 946918 04 X Pb £3.95
ISBN 0 946918 00 7 Hb £8.95

Language

Caribbean & African Languages:
Social History Language, Literature and Education

by Morgan Dalphinis

ISBN 0 946918 06 6 Pb £6.95
ISBN 0 946918 07 4 Hb £16.95

Language and Liberation:
Creole Language Politics in the Caribbean

by Hubert Devonish

ISBN 0 946918 27 9 Pb £5.95
ISBN 0 946918 27 8 Hb £9.95

New Poetry

Because The Dawn Breaks!
Poems Dedicated to the Grenadian People

by Merle Collins
With Introduction by Ngũgĩ Wa Thiong'o

ISBN 0 946918 08 2 Pb £3.95
ISBN 0 946918 09 0 Hb £8.95

For Those Who Will Come After!

by Morgan Dalphinis

ISBN 0 946918 10 4 Pb £3.95
ISBN 0 946918 11 2 Hb £8.95

Word Rhythms From the Life of A Woman

by Elean Thomas

ISBN 0 946918 40 6 Pb £3.95
ISBN 0 946918 41 4 Hb £8.95

Rapso Explosion

by Bro. Resistance

ISBN 0 946918 34 1 Pb £3.95